Dear P

STEP INTO READING® will help your child get there. The program offers five steps to reading success. Each step includes fun stories and colorful art or photographs. In addition to original fiction and books with favorite characters, there are Step into Reading Non-Fiction Readers, Phonics Readers and Boxed Sets, Sticker Readers, and Comic Readers—a complete literacy program with something to interest every child.

Learning to Read, Step by Step!

Ready to Read   Preschool–Kindergarten
• big type and easy words • rhyme and rhythm • picture clues
For children who know the alphabet and are eager to begin reading.

Reading with Help   Preschool–Grade 1
• basic vocabulary • short sentences • simple stories
For children who recognize familiar words and sound out new words with help.

Reading on Your Own   Grades 1–3
• engaging characters • easy-to-follow plots • popular topics
For children who are ready to read on their own.

Reading Paragraphs   Grades 2–3
• challenging vocabulary • short paragraphs • exciting stories
For newly independent readers who read simple sentences with confidence.

Ready for Chapters   Grades 2–4
• chapters • longer paragraphs • full-color art
For children who want to take the plunge into chapter books but still like colorful pictures.

STEP INTO READING® is designed to
reading experience. The grade levels ar   ress
through the steps at their own speed, d   ding.

Remember, a lifetime love of reading st

All rights reserved. Published in the United States by Random House Children's Books,
a division of Penguin Random House LLC, 1745 Broadway, New York, NY 10019, and in
Canada by Penguin Random House Canada Limited, Toronto.

Step into Reading, Random House, and the Random House colophon are registered trademarks
of Penguin Random House LLC.

Visit us on the Web!
StepIntoReading.com
rhcbooks.com
dckids.com

Educators and librarians, for a variety of teaching tools, visit us at RHTeachersLibrarians.com

ISBN 978-0-525-64851-2 (trade) — ISBN 978-0-525-64852-9 (lib. bdg.)
ISBN 978-0-525-64853-6 (ebook)

Printed in the United States of America

10 9 8 7 6 5 4 3 2 1

THE SECRET OF SHAZAM!

by Christy Webster
illustrated by Erik Doescher

Random House 🏠 New York

Meet Billy.
He is a nice,
helpful boy.

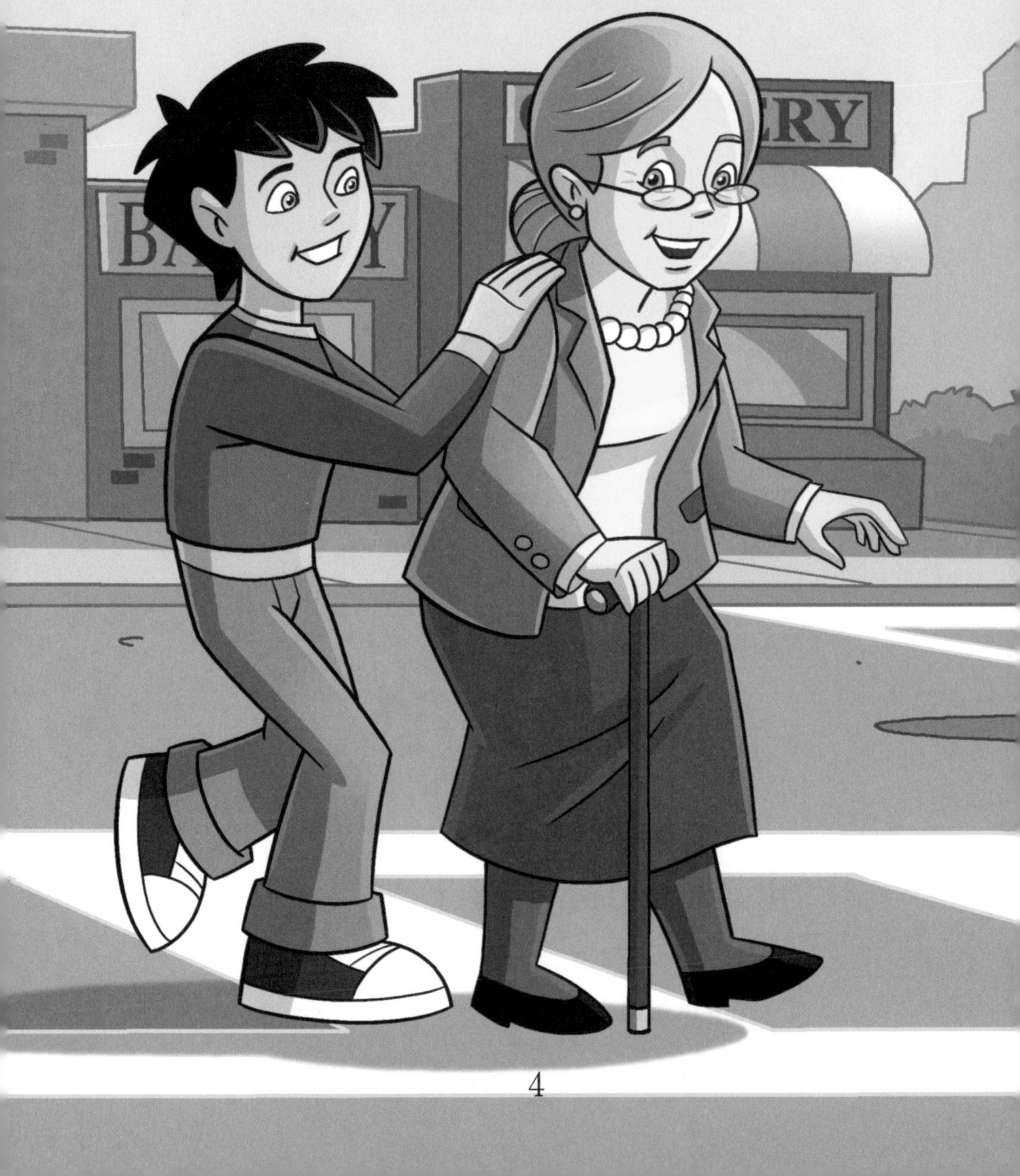

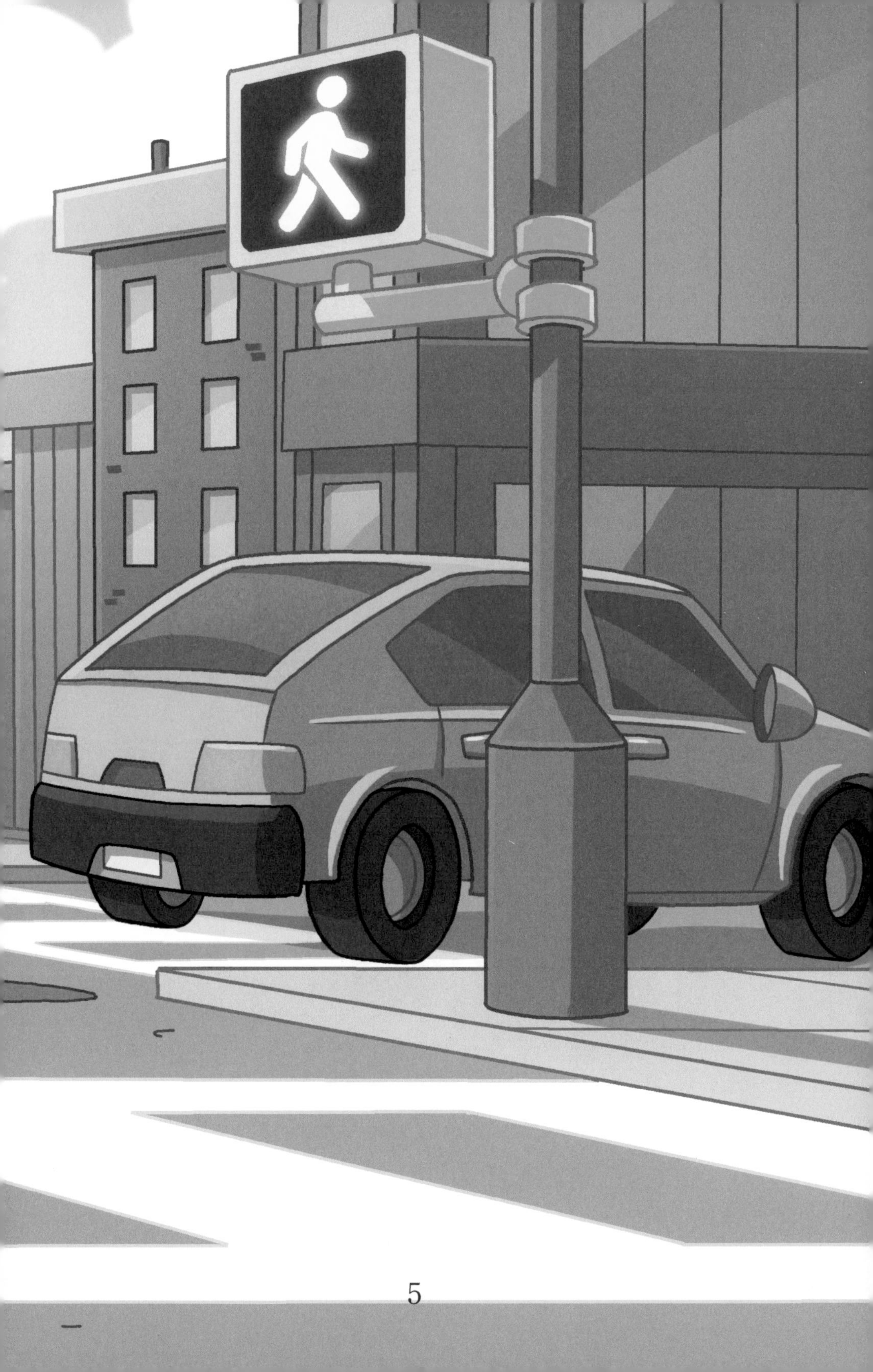

One day,
Billy meets
a wizard.

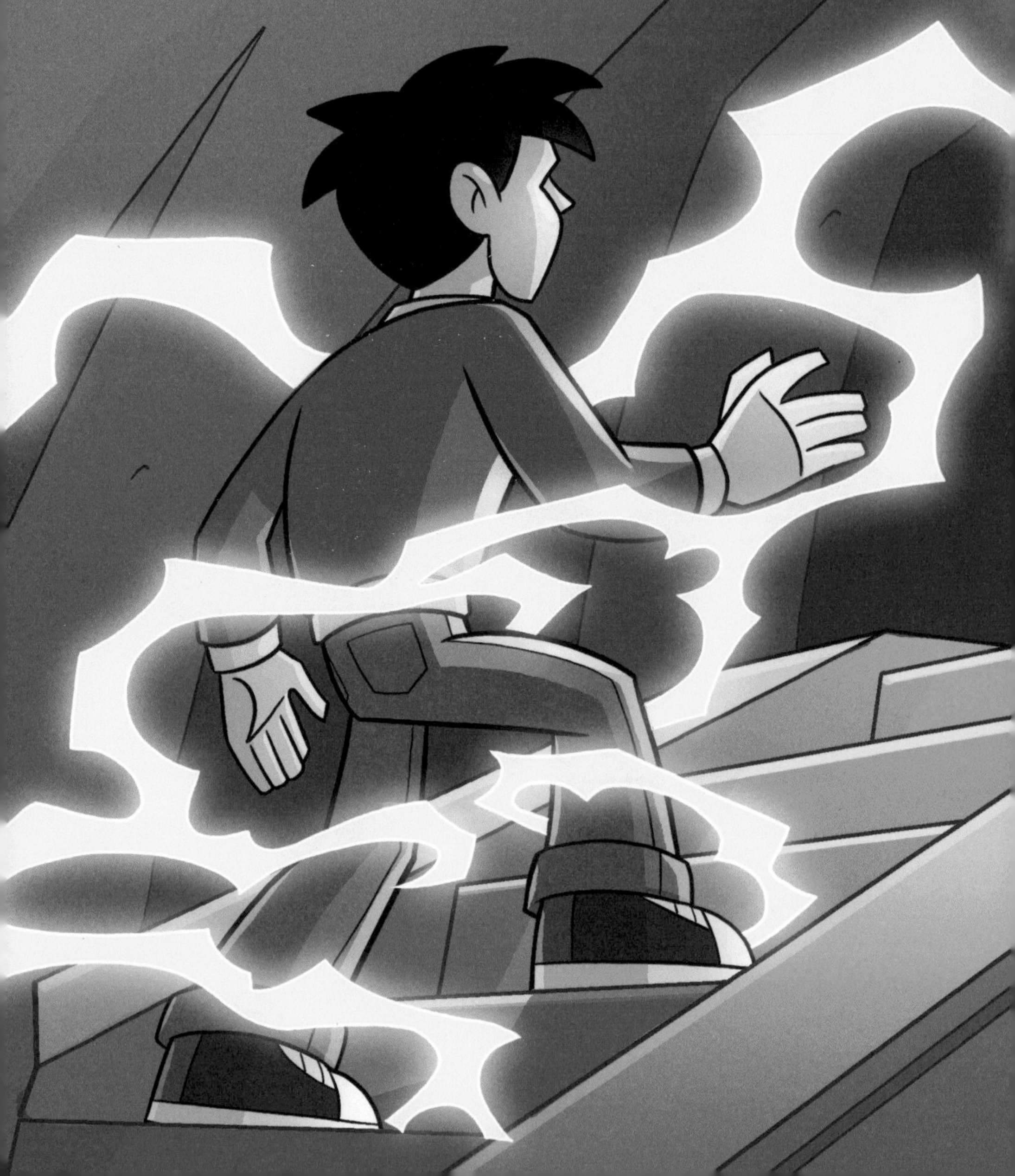

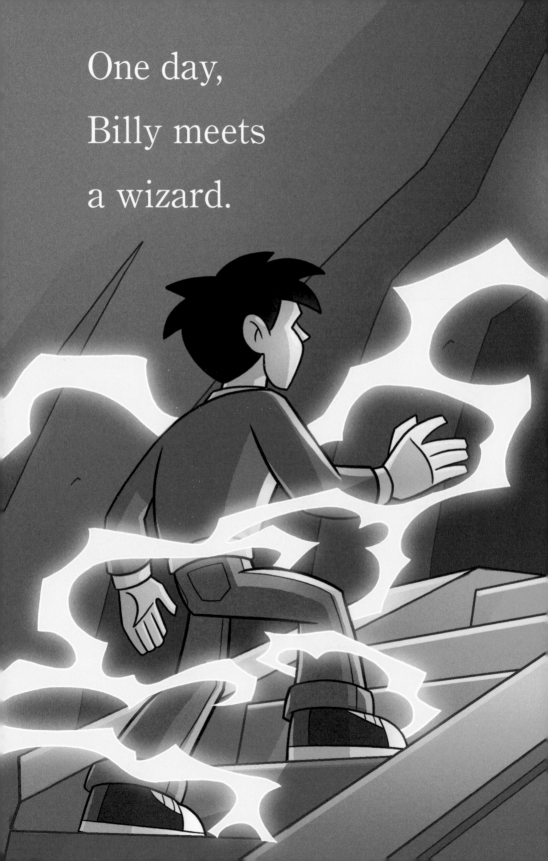

The wizard gives Billy
magical powers.

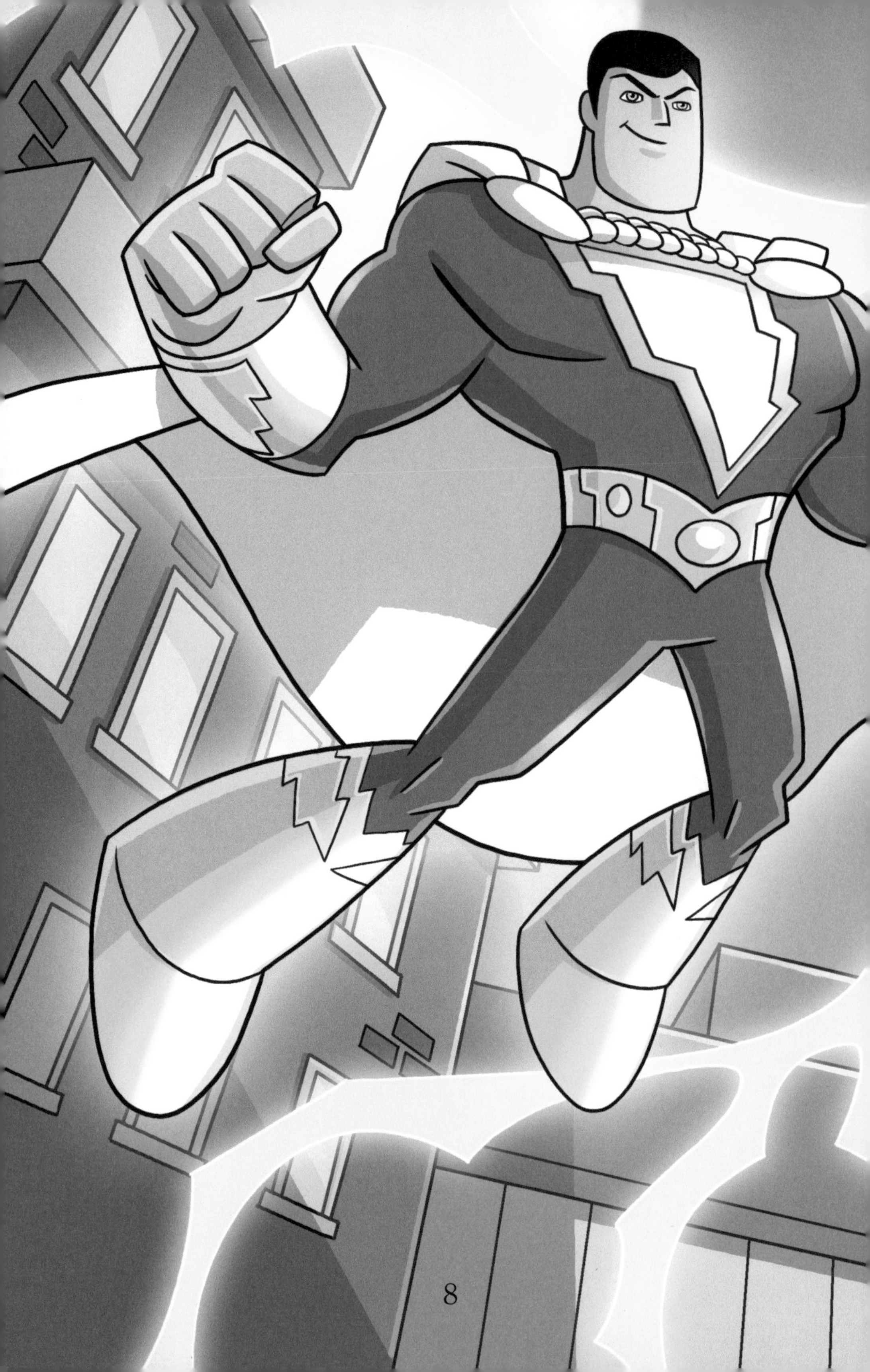

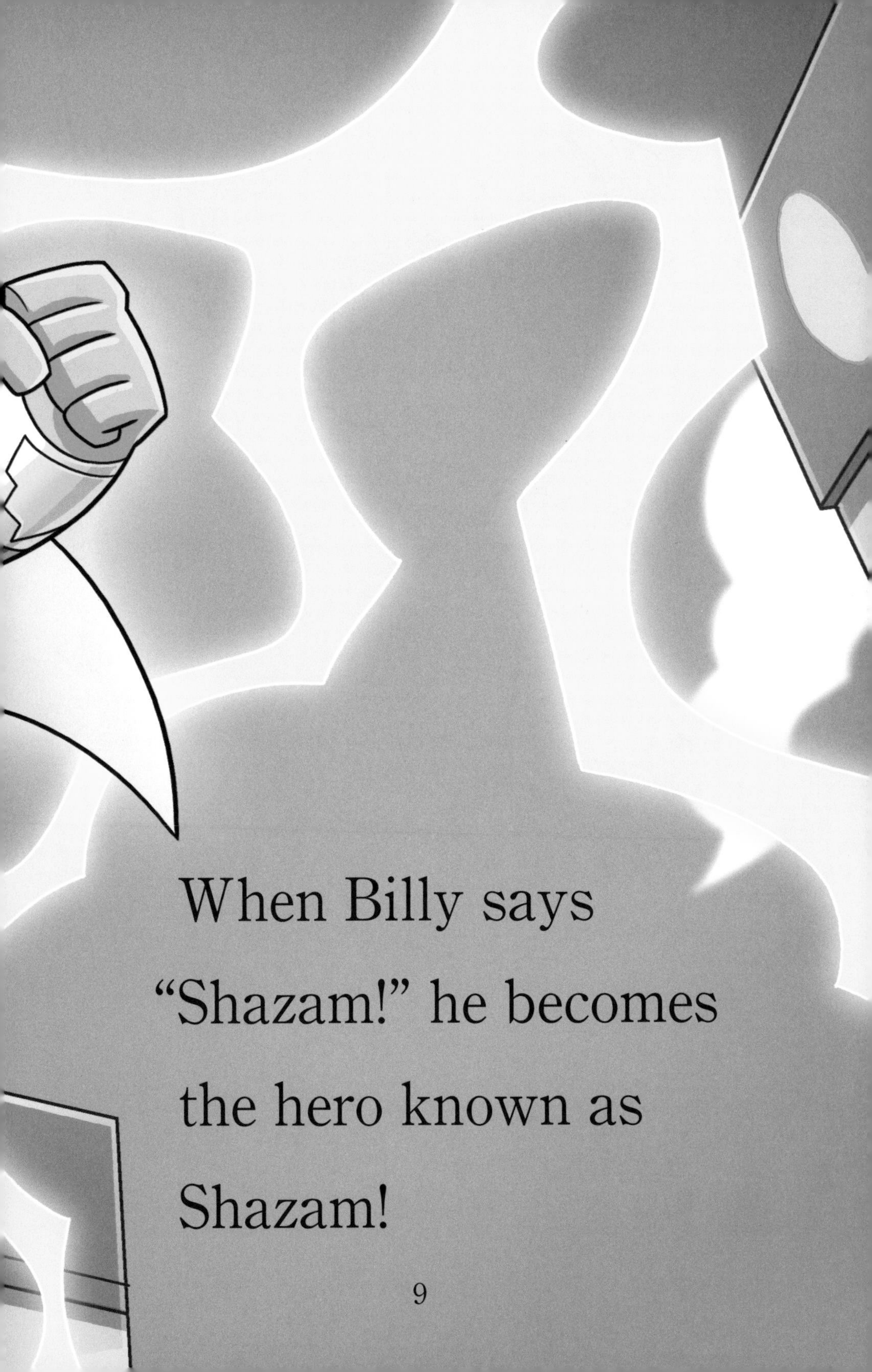

When Billy says "Shazam!" he becomes the hero known as Shazam!

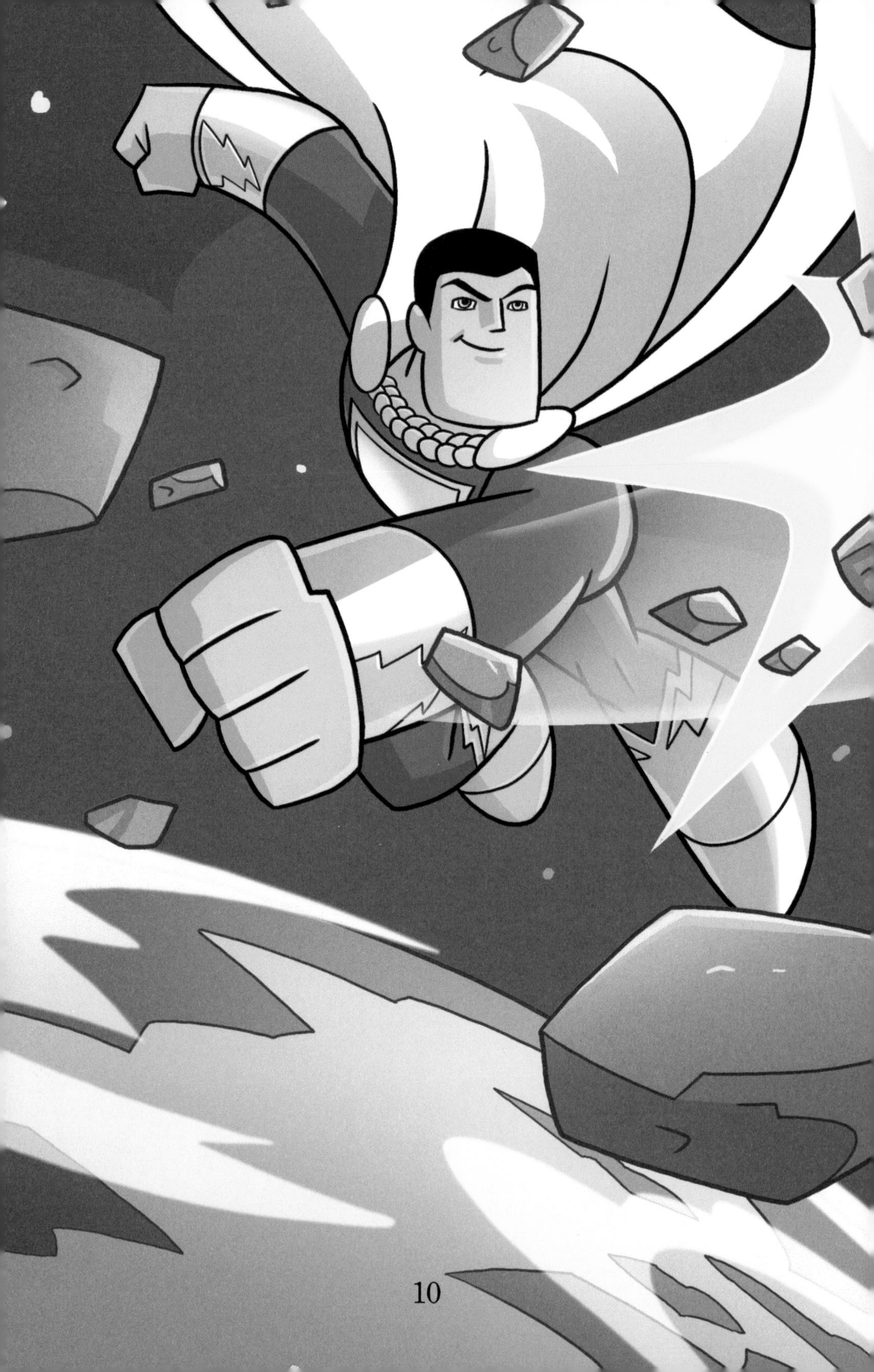

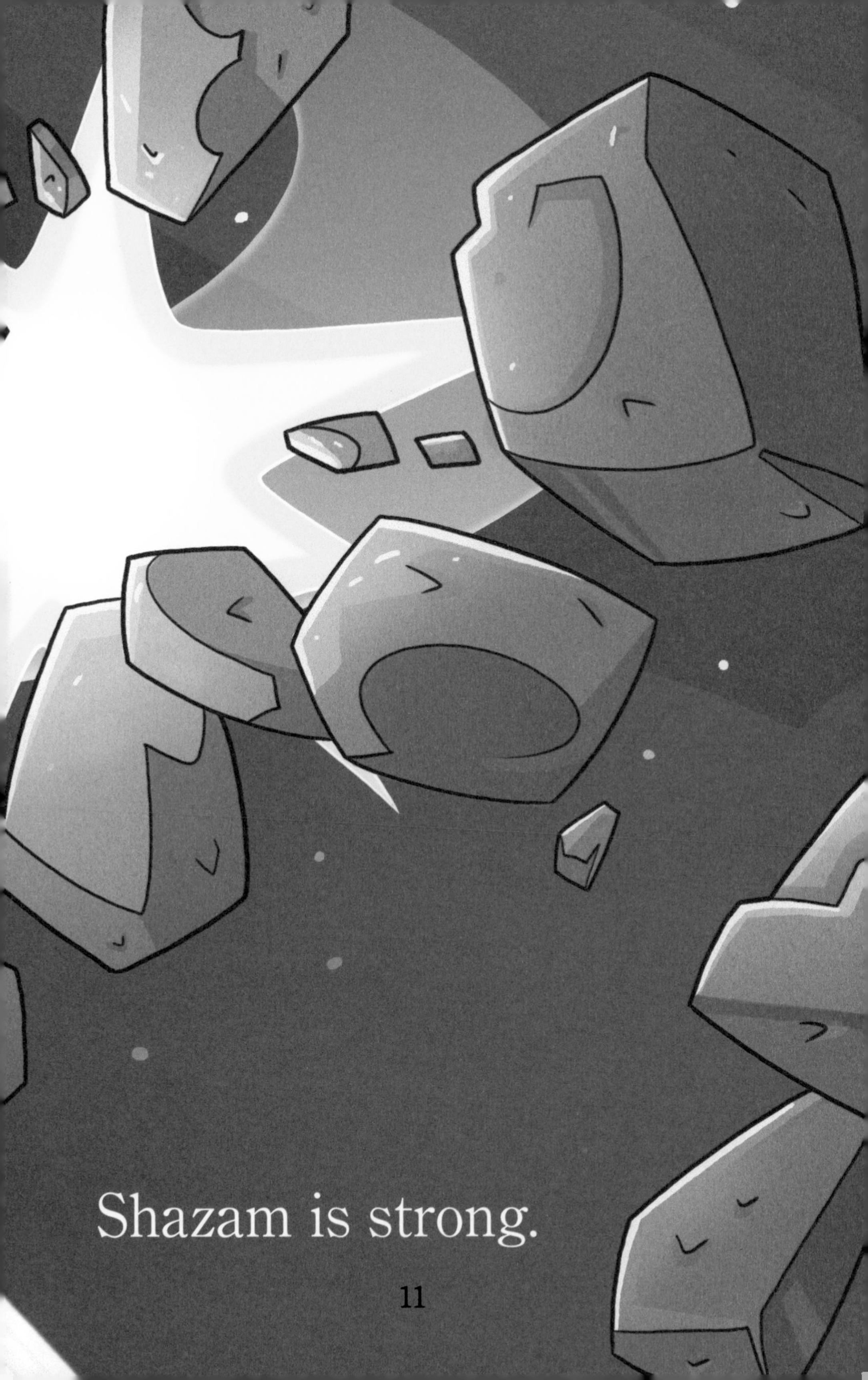

Shazam is strong.

Shazam is fast.

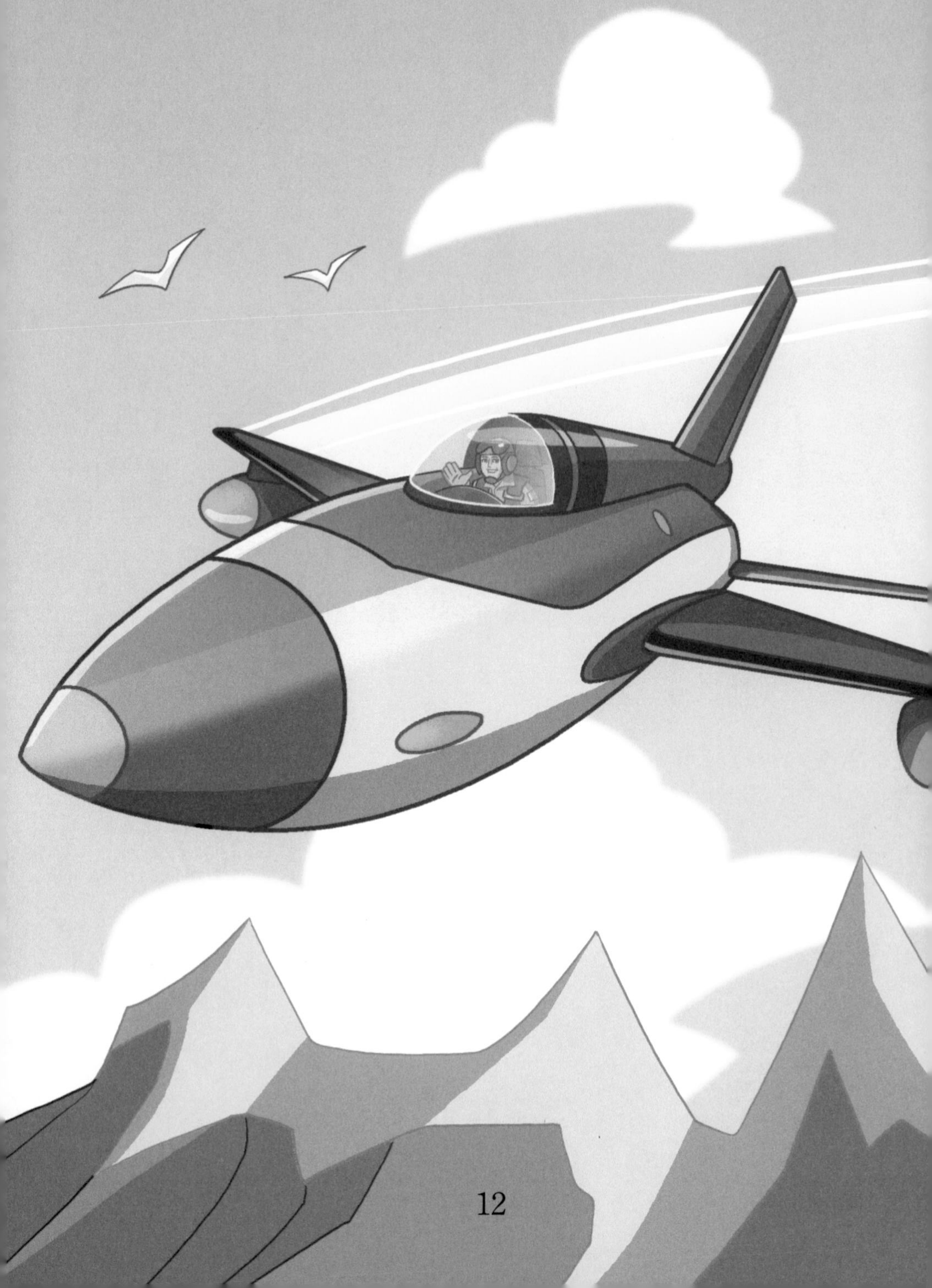

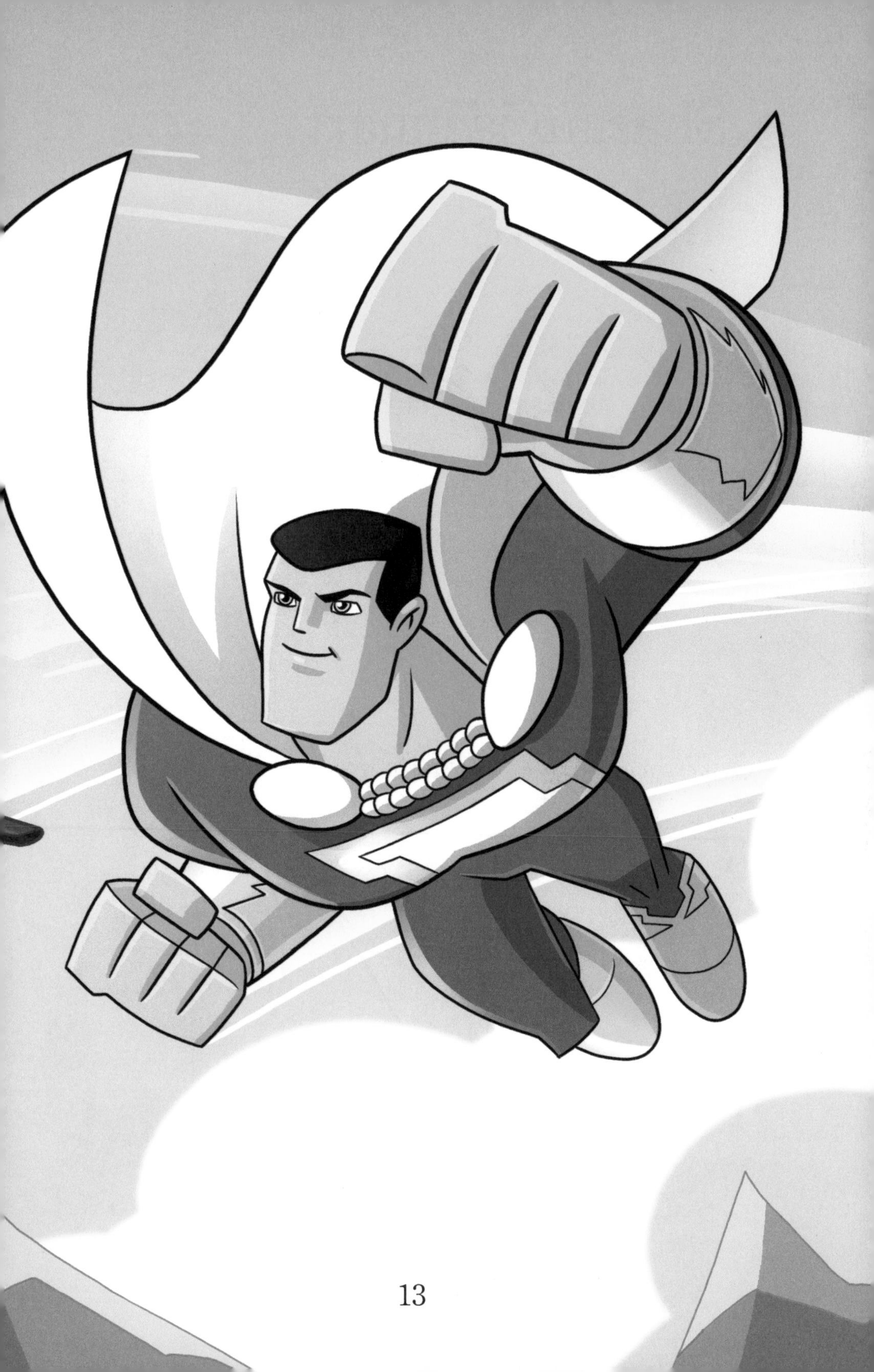

Shazam is smart

and brave.

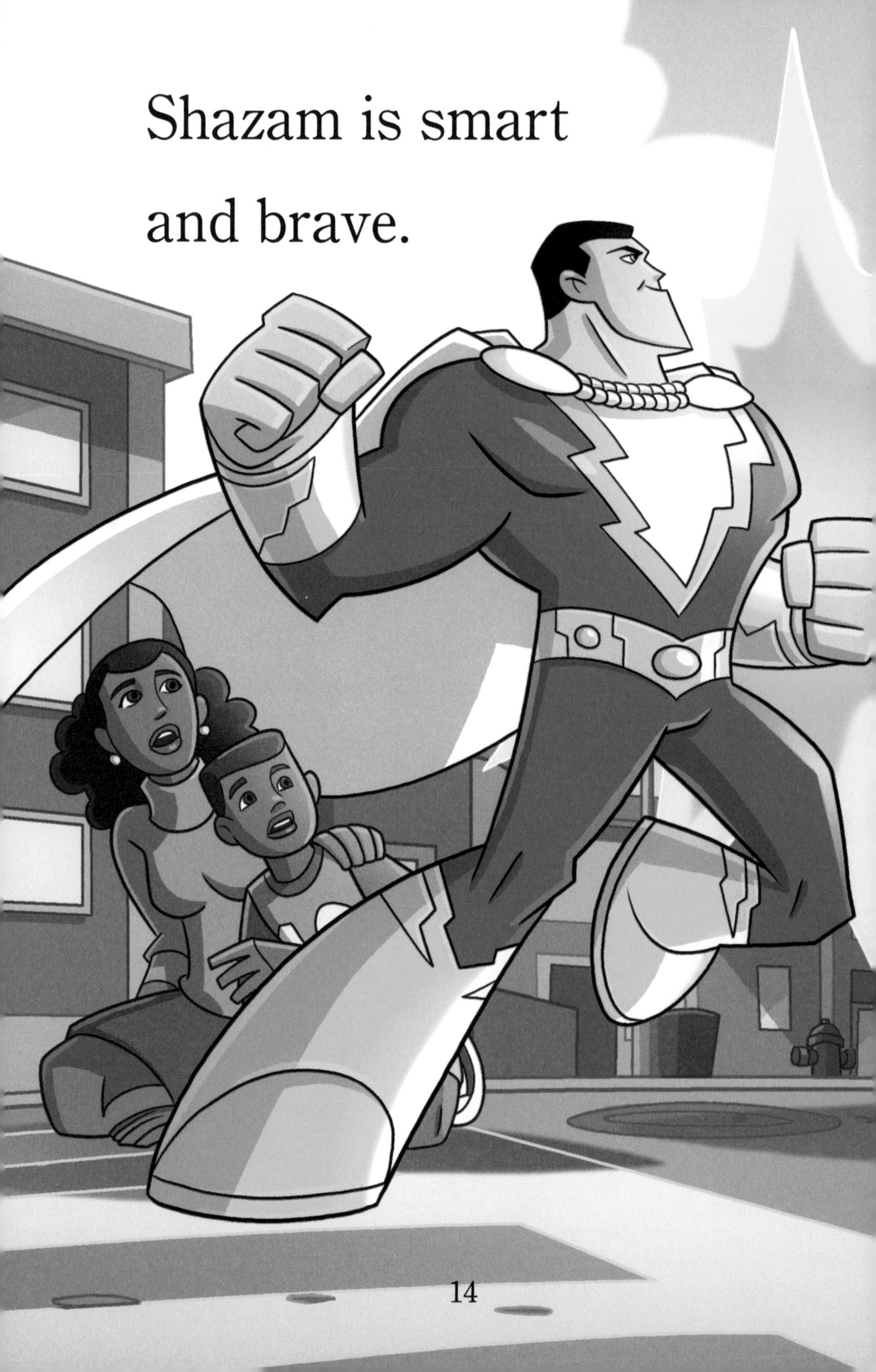

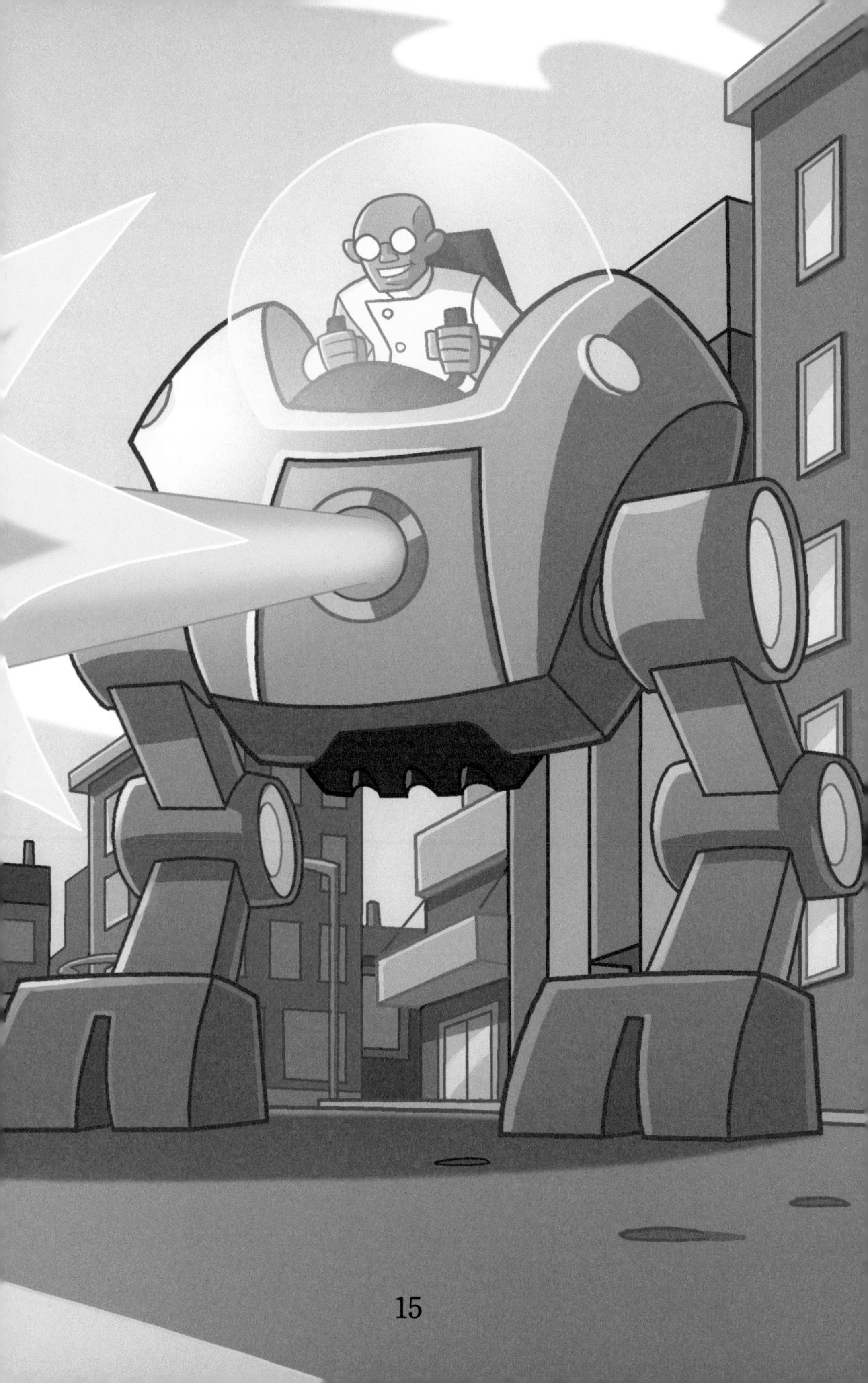

Shazam catches crooks!

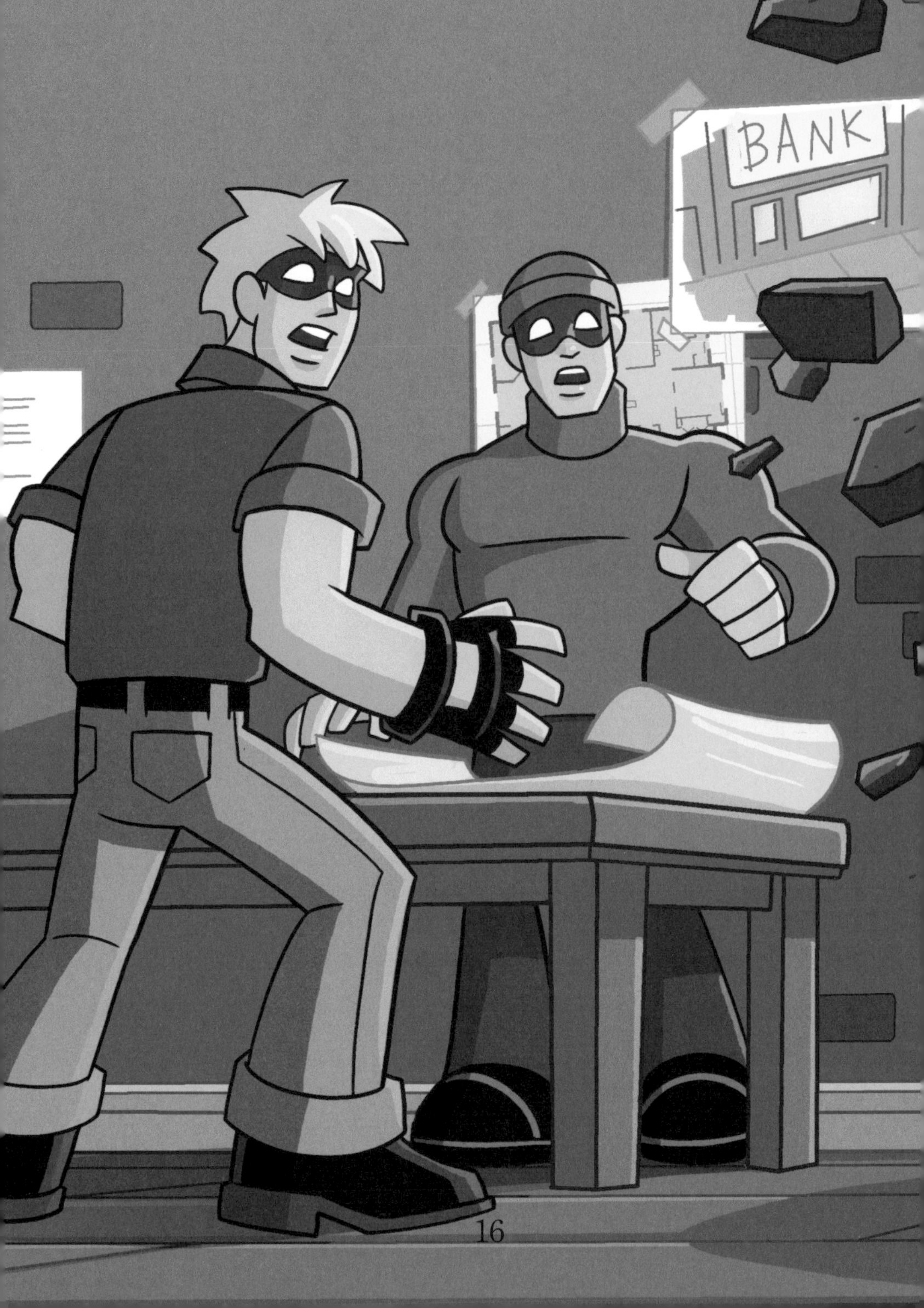
BANK

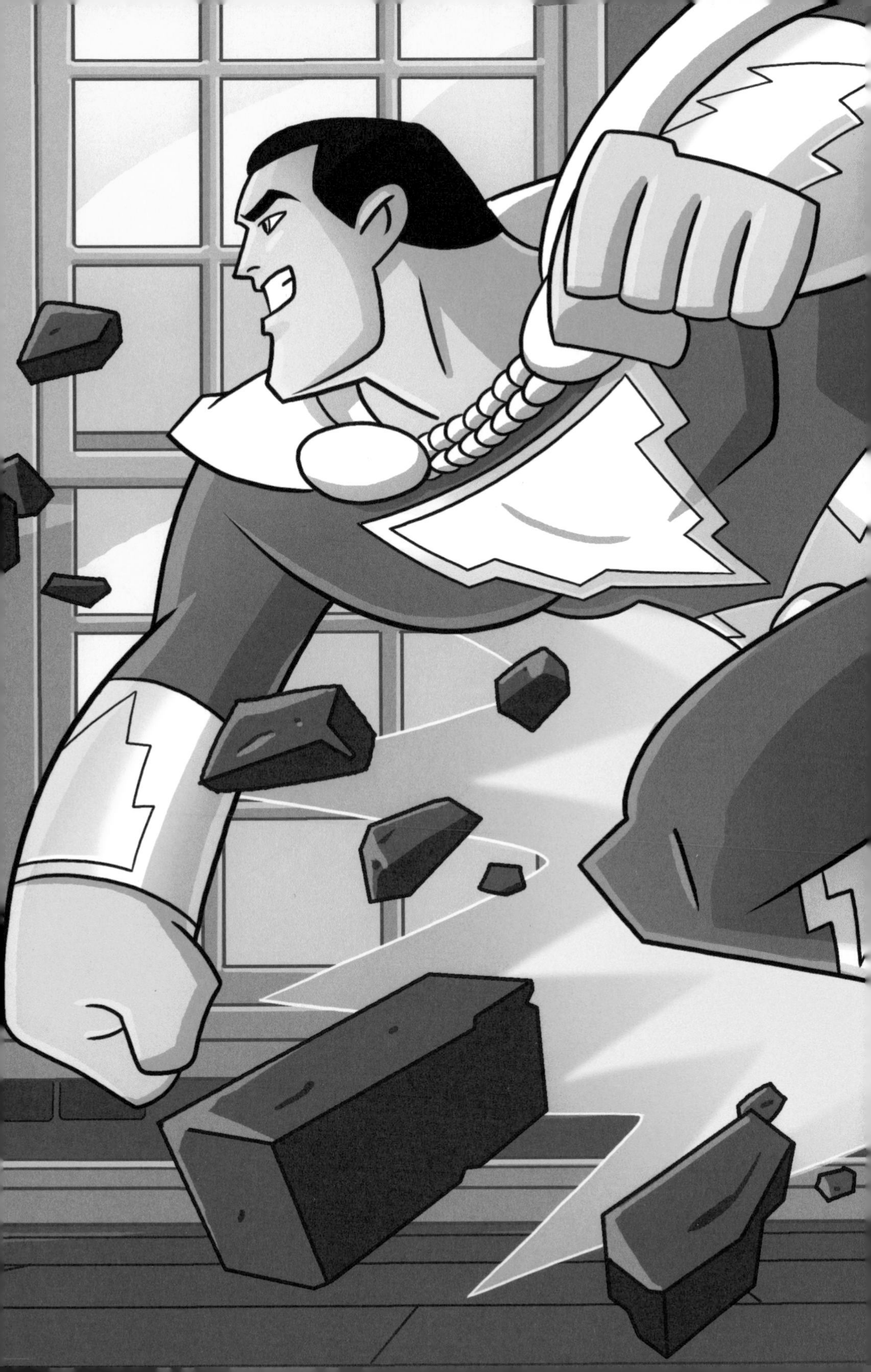

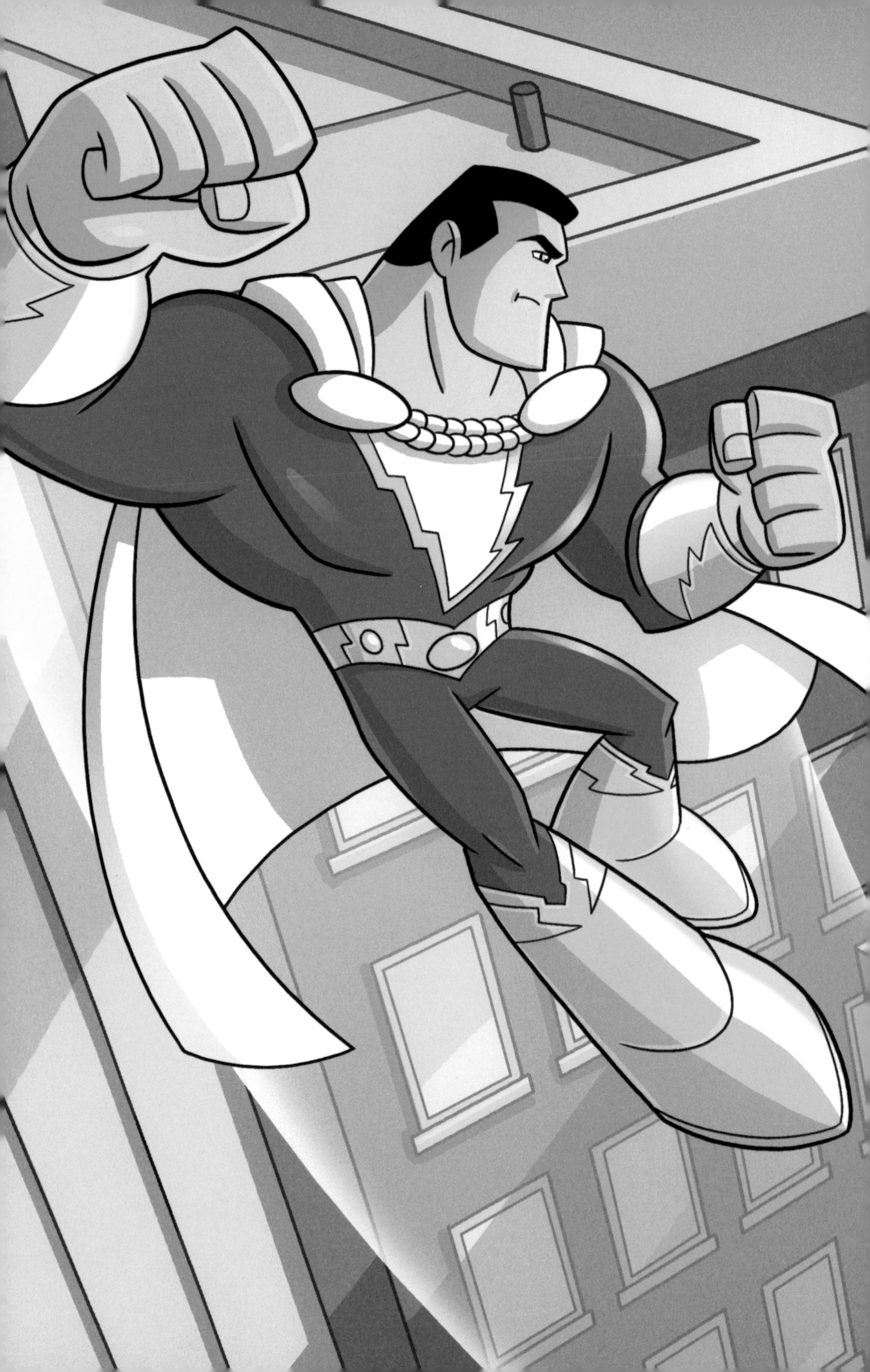

Black Adam has powers,
just like Shazam.
But he is bad.

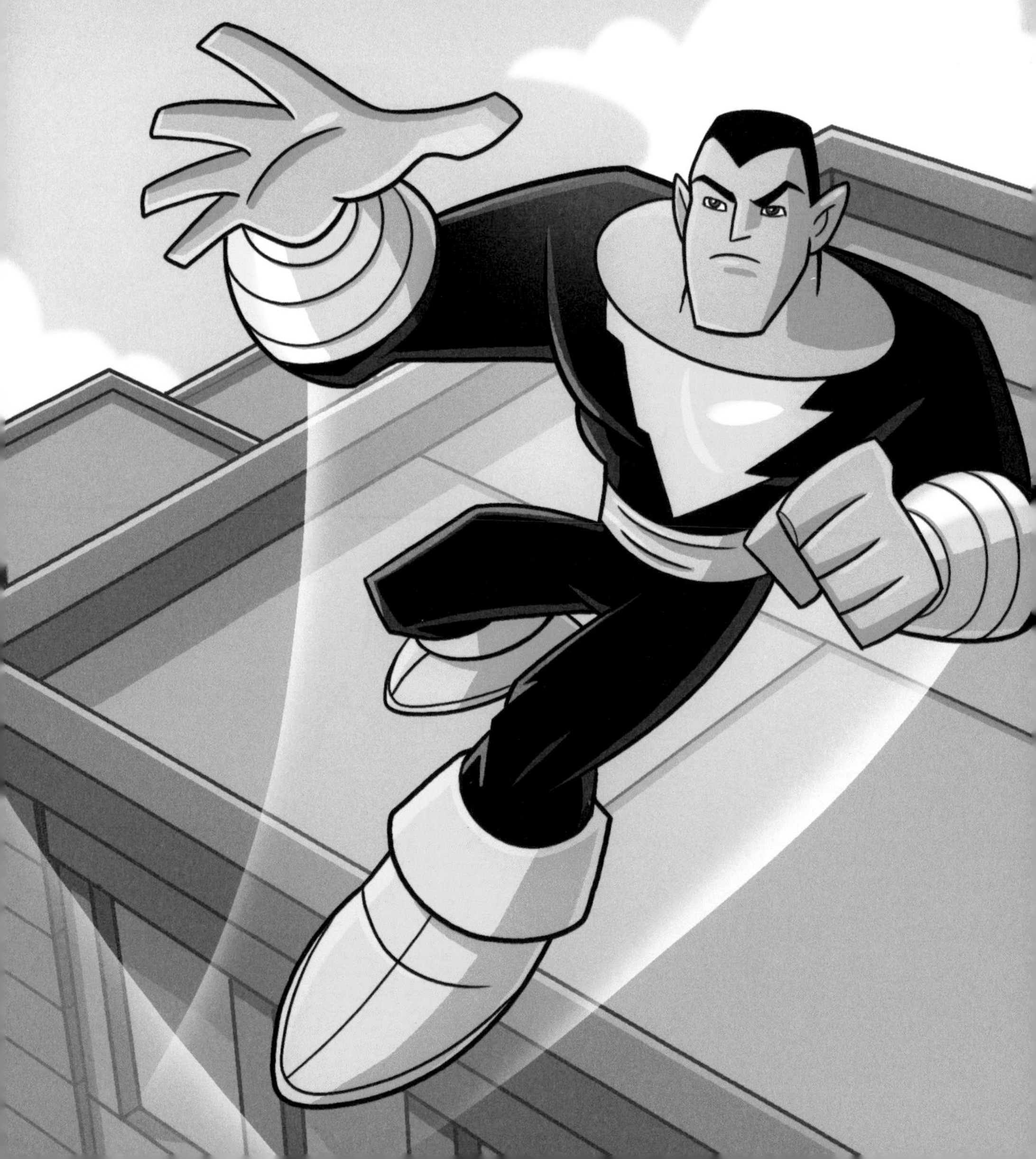

Shazam uses the power of lightning to defeat him!

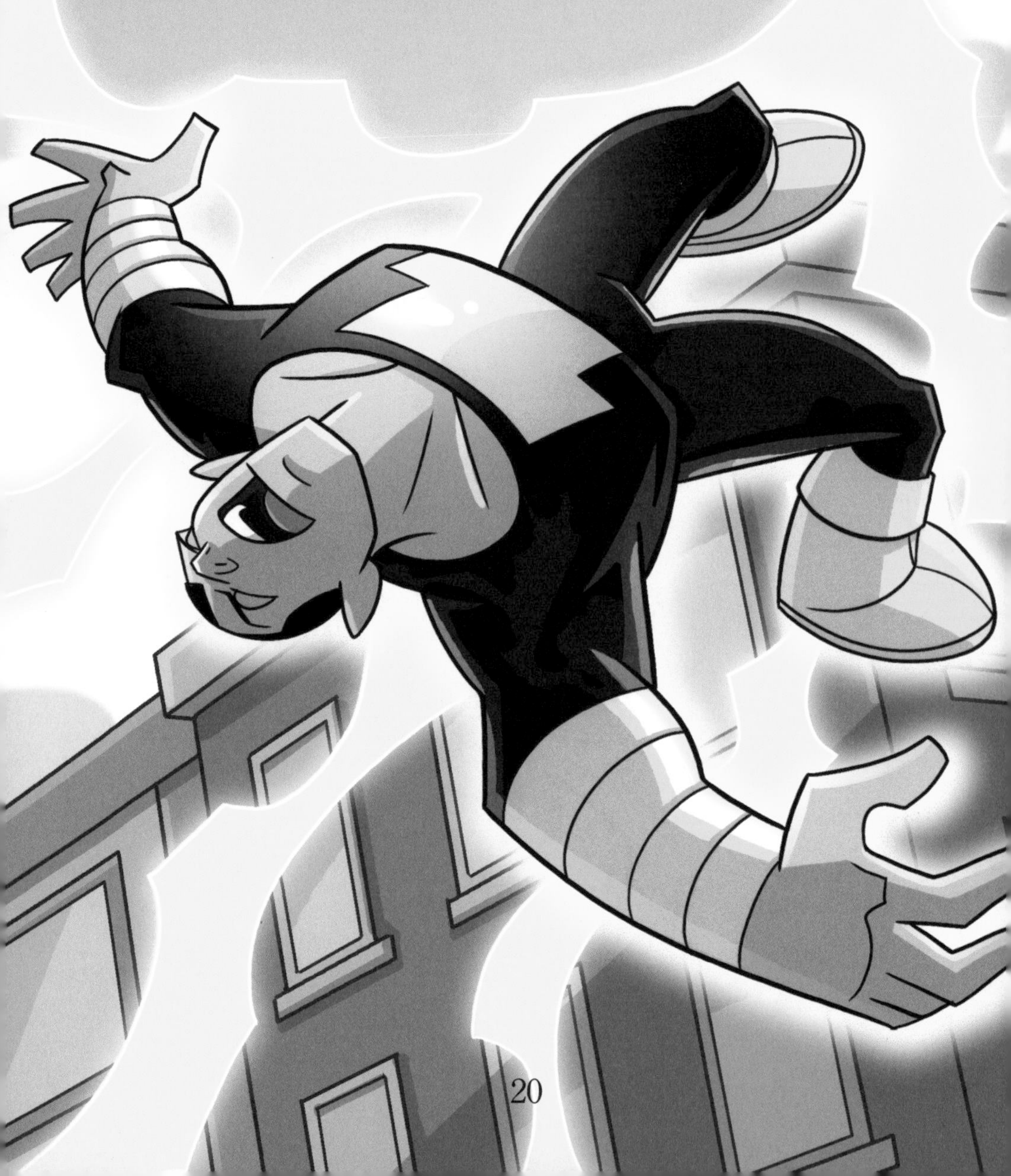

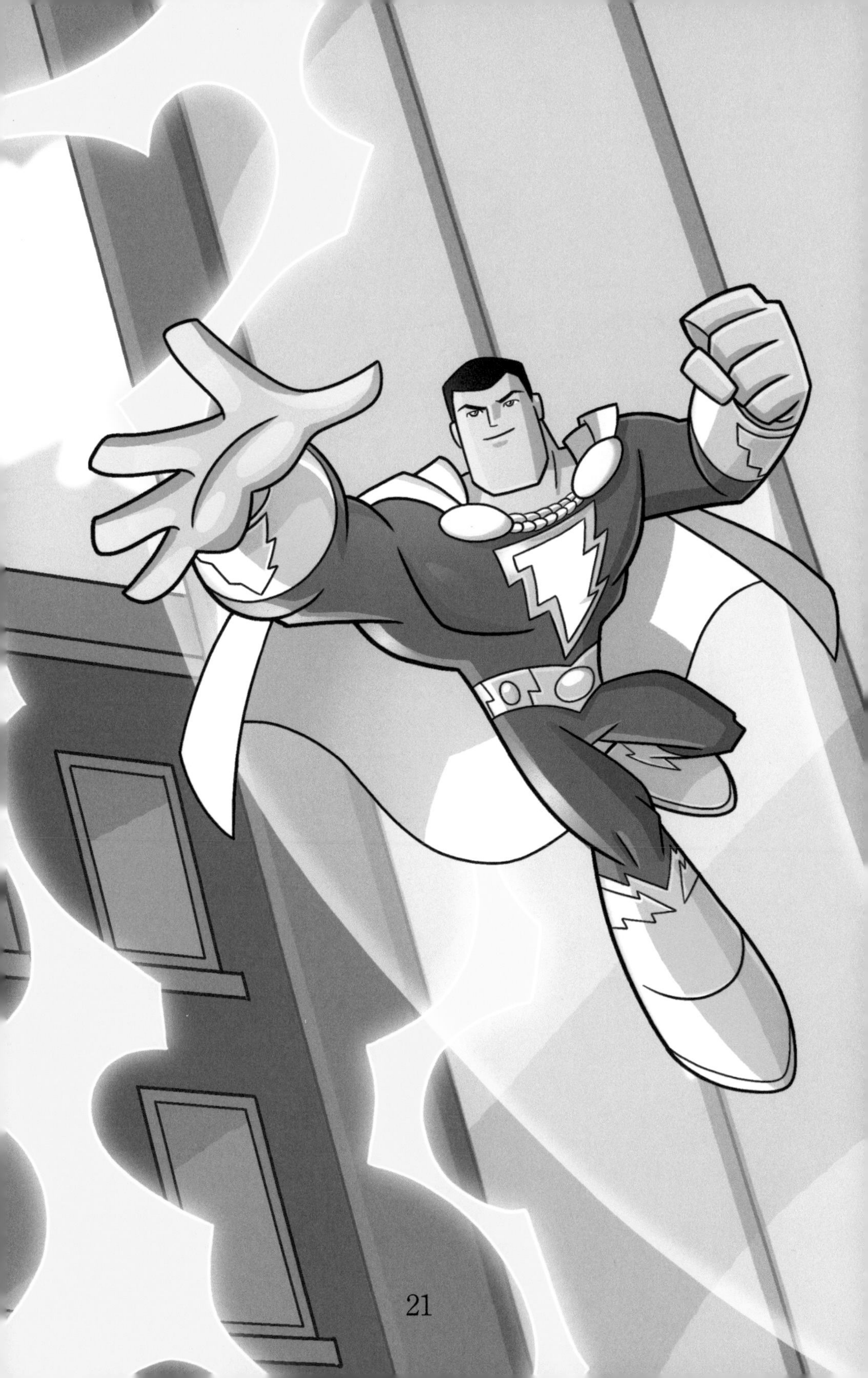

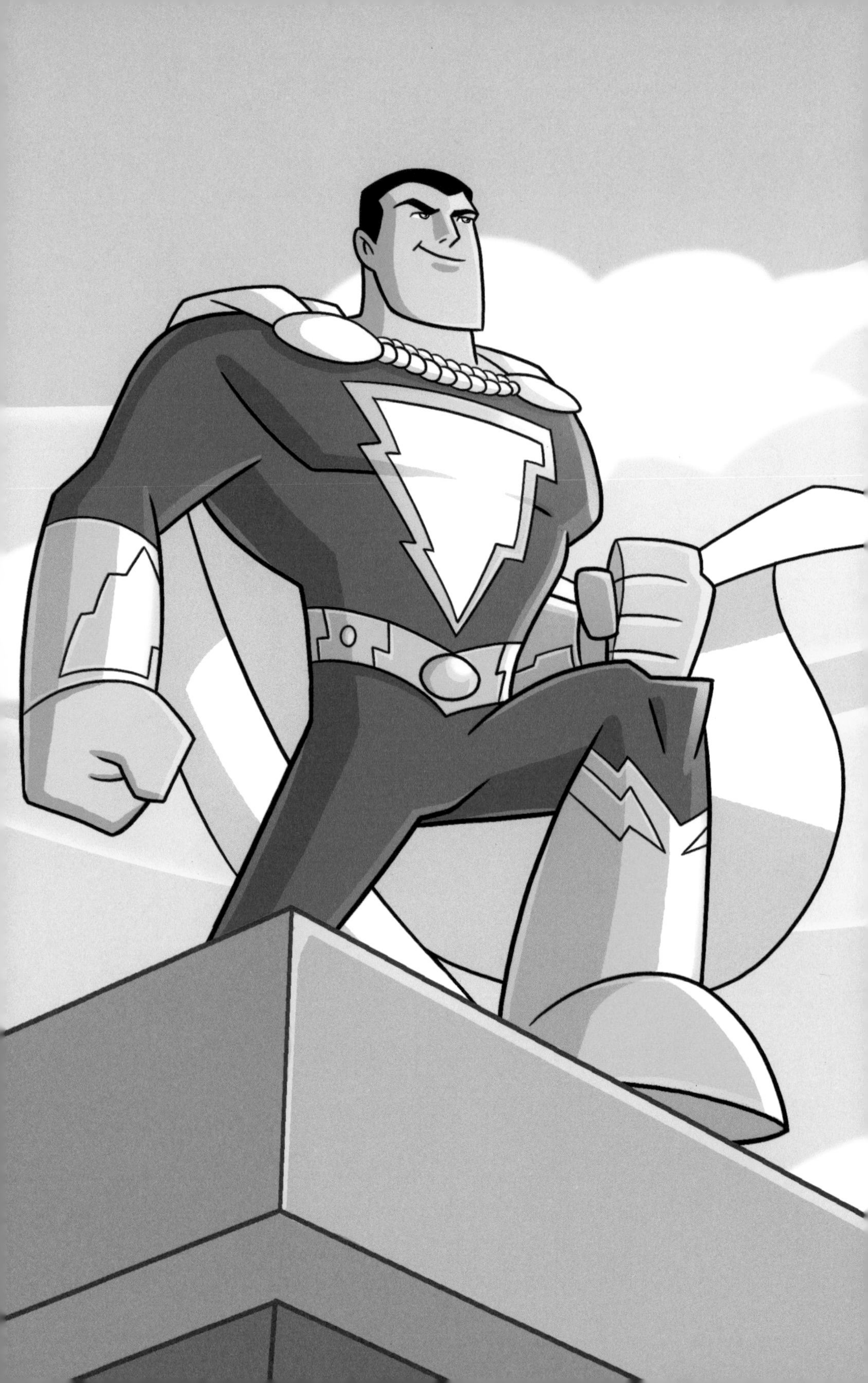

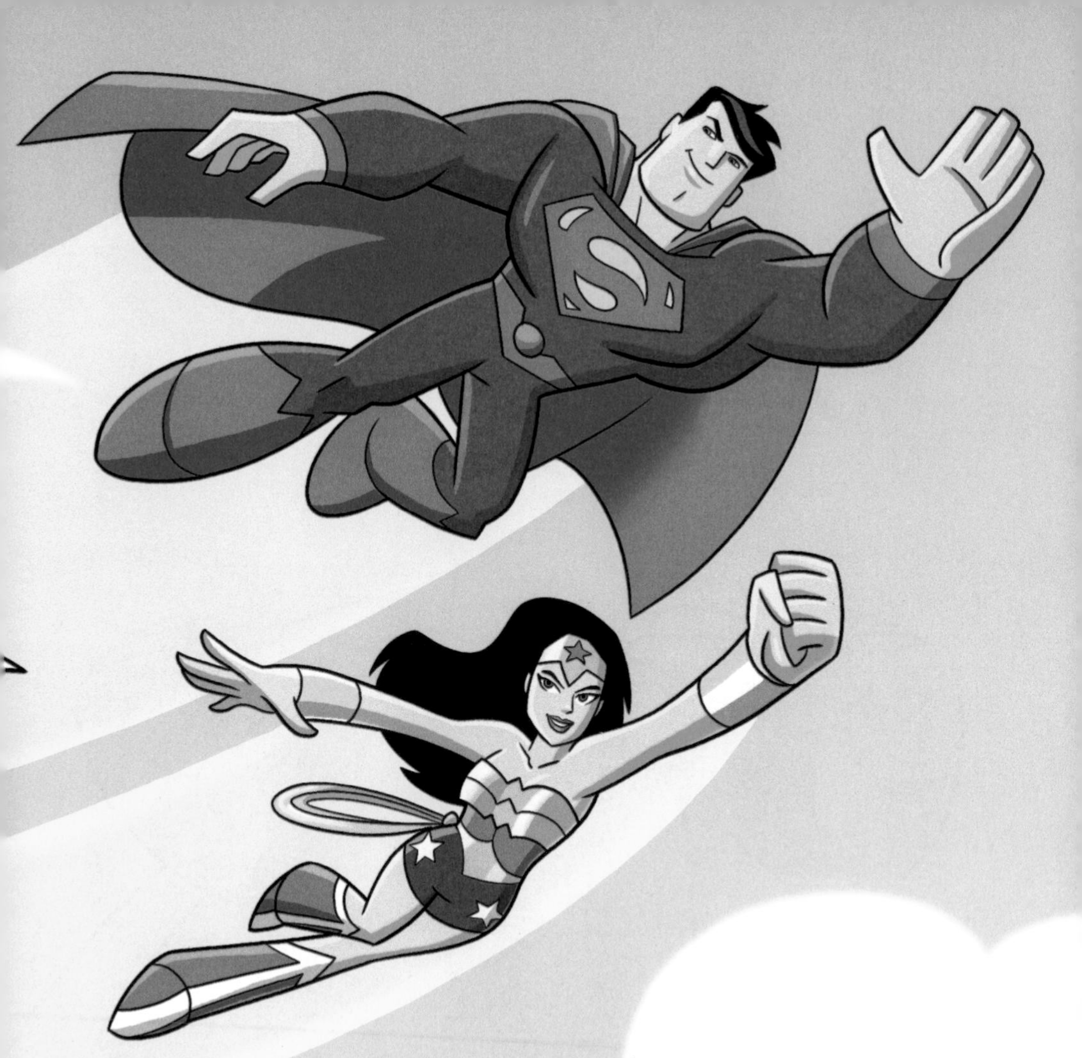

Shazam also has
amazing friends,
like Superman and
Wonder Woman!

He is a true hero.

"SHAZAM!"

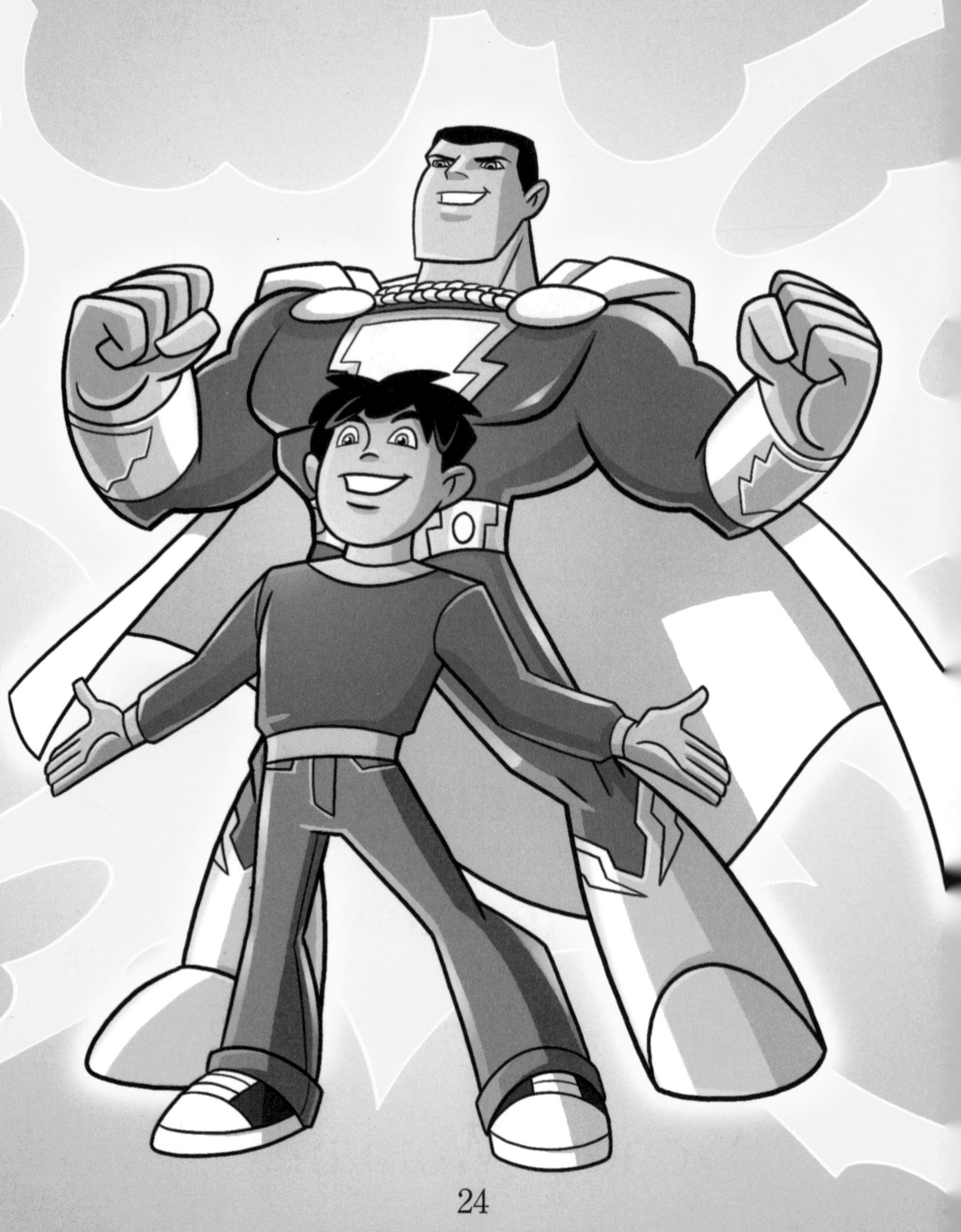